Disney

Hundred-Acre Adventures

Lost Kite

Ladybird

It was a very windy day in the Hundred-Acre Wood. The leaves were swirling round and round, higher and higher into the sky. Tigger was looking out from his house when he saw a beautiful kite floating over towards him.

'Yippee! A kite! Tiggers love kites! Kites can fly even higher than I can bounce!' yelled Tigger. Just then he had a thought.

'Hmmm,' he wondered. 'Didn't Christopher Robin give Tigger a kite?' He rushed inside to search for his kite.

'When you hold a kite, you can bounce even higher!' Tigger said. 'But first you have to have a kite and some wind. And today we have both!'

Tigger searched and searched. But all he found was a hammer, a bugle and a shoe. There was no kite.

'Oh, kite, where are you?' called Tigger. 'Kite! Answer me!'

Of course there was no reply.

'It is a kiteless home, and a kiteless home is like a windy day without wind. Or like a Tigger not wanting to bounce,' sighed Tigger sadly. 'I am a poor kiteless Tigger.'

Just then Tigger heard a little voice calling to him.

'What is happening, Tigger?'

It was Piglet!

Tigger looked down. All of his friends were there, but not his kite.

'Ah! Piglet. Ah! Rabbit. Ah! Owl. Ah! Pooh,' moaned Tigger.

'Ah! Eeyore,' Eeyore added.

'My kite has disappeared,' wailed Tigger.

'Disappeared?' Owl repeated as he pushed his glasses up his beak. 'Let's try and understand what you are talking about, Tigger. Have you lost your kite, or can't you find it?'

'I have lost it, because I can't find it!' said Tigger.

Owl listened to Tigger and knew that it was a day when his wise words were needed.

'Let me explain,' began Owl, 'either the kite is lost because you can't find it. Or you can't find it because it is lost. Or it may not be lost at all! Maybe you have only forgotten where you put it. I therefore declare that you have to remember where you put it!'

Tigger was now very confused.

'I don't think Tigger actually put his kite away,' declared Rabbit. 'That would be too good to be true. And, by the way, if he had put it away, why would he now be looking for it? Hmmph!'

'I am not looking for it,' replied Tigger. 'I cannot find it!'

'Let's start again,' sighed Owl. 'When did you last see your kite, Tigger?'

Tigger thought long and hard.

'I saw it with me,' he mumbled.

'Where were you?' questioned Owl.

Tigger had to think a little more.

'Erm, in the Heather Field… or near the Stony Hill… or by the Honey Tree…' Tigger couldn't really remember.

'Tigger, I am sure you would never have left your kite outside,' said Pooh. 'Have you searched your house from tippity top to bottomy bottom?'

Tigger scratched his head and thought hard.

'You're right, Pooh! I forgot to look under the armchair, and in the basketball net!'

Several bounces later, Tigger was back. He was looking sadder than ever.

'No, it's lost, completely lost!' he wailed.

'Poor Tigger,' cried Piglet as he hid his tears in his basket.

'Don't be sad,' said Pooh kindly. He told his friend to remember all the wonderful bounces he used to do with his kite!

'When I remember all the delicious honey I have eaten, it is like eating it all over again.'

'Pooh is right,' Piglet added. 'It's still your kite, even if it is lost!'

'These beautiful memories belong to you forever,' Owl concluded. 'It is wonderful!'

'Wonderful,' Tigger repeated sadly.

'You should be happy to have lost your kite,' Eeyore said. 'If I had lost mine, you would all be rolling on the floor laughing. I am glad nobody ever offered me a kite. Nor anything else, by the way…'

'That's right,' Pooh cried. 'What matters most is that Christopher Robin once gave you a present.'

These kind words brought back a smile on Tigger's face.

'That's fine!' Owl was delighted. 'You seem much happier, you will be all right!'

'But I'm not all right,' Eeyore said, sadly, 'I don't have a kite.'

'Neither do we!' replied Rabbit. 'Now, this kite must be somewhere, it didn't just fly away!' The friends began to search again for the lost kite.

'Well, Rabbit, I think you have hit on it. I think the kite has flown away!' said Owl. 'Look! Tigger's window is open!'

A long silence followed Owl's wise words. Pooh scratched his head.

'And where exactly would a kite fly to?' Pooh asked. 'If I were a kite, I would have flown to the Honey Tree.'

'Or to my garden to admire my vegetables,' Rabbit added.

'Or to my shed, to laugh about me,' Eeyore moaned.

'As for me, I don't know,' Piglet said sadly. 'But let's go and find out!'

But the friends didn't find the lost kite near the Honey Tree, nor in Rabbit's garden, nor at Eeyore's.

The gang of friends were all very sad as they sat down by the river.

'But where could it have gone?' Rabbit wondered.

'I will never hold its string again,' said Tigger gloomily.

'What if it has fallen into the river?' Piglet asked.

They all stared at the water rolling away. No kite!

'Dear Tigger,' said Pooh as they headed back. 'I have lost a lot of honey in my tummy, and somehow the bees always provided some more!'

'And I have lost lots of vegetables because of hail and frost,' Rabbit added, 'and they always grow back!'

'As for me…' added Piglet. 'Oh bother! I've lost my basket.'

Tigger went over to comfort Piglet.

'Calm down, little Piglet,' said Tigger, kindly.
'Tell us if your basket was full or empty?'

'Well… it was empty!' cried Piglet in relief.
'I hadn't collected any acorns yet.'

'So it's not so bad,' Tigger concluded. 'And, tell
me, can't you find it, or have you lost it? As Owl
would ask!'

Just then, Piglet
remembered that he
left his basket near
the bridge. All the
gang ran with Piglet
to try and find the
missing basket.

But when they reached the river, the basket was gone – the wind had blown it away.

'Don't worry, Piglet,' said Rabbit to reassure his friend. 'I have an almost exact same basket for you at my house!'

'Oh thank you, Rabbit,' said Piglet. 'You're so kind!'

'A kite and a basket! Me, oh my! This wind is quite a character,' Tigger laughed. 'Mr Wind has certainly played some good tricks on us today!'